P9-BJR-130

LILIES, RABBITS, and PAINTED EGGS

The Story of the Easter Symbols

by EDNA BARTH
illustrated by URSULA ARNDT

THE SEABURY PRESS · NEW YORK

The excerpt from Akhnaton's "Hymn to the Sun,"
which appeared in *Man and the Sun* by Jacquetta
Hawkes, Random House, Inc., copyright © 1962 by the
author, is reprinted by permission of the publisher.

Text copyright © 1970 by Edna Barth
Illustrations copyright © 1970 by Ursula Arndt
Library of Congress Catalog Card Number: 74-97033

All rights reserved. No part of this book may be
reproduced in any form, except by a reviewer,
without the permission of the publisher.

Designed by Carol Basen
Printed in the United States of America
Third Printing

Contents

18,444

Pur 1973

J
394.26
B

*P*ainted *eggs, candy eggs, bunnies, newborn* chicks, lambs, white lilies, new clothes. All these stand for Easter just as angels and reindeer stand for Christmas, or witches and pumpkins for Halloween.

Weeks before Easter some of its symbols, like Easter baskets filled with beautiful eggs, or tall white lilies, appear in shop windows for all to see. Others, such as a single tall white lighted candle, are seen only in a church. Still others, such as roast lamb or ham on an Easter dinner table, are found only in peoples' homes.

From one part of the country to another and from land to land the Easter flowers or Easter eggs may differ a little. But an Easter egg or plant, a new Easter hat, or any other Easter symbol means the same thing wherever it is found. And each one has a story that goes back hundreds or even thousands of years to the beginning of the Christian religion or long before.

5

Easter, a Season and a Day

The Christian religion began with Jesus Christ nearly two thousand years ago. Jesus was believed to be the son of God, who lived on earth, died, and was brought to life again by God. Christmas marks the birth of Jesus. Easter celebrates his resurrection.

Easter, in the northern hemisphere, always comes in the spring but not always on the same day. It is called a movable feast. What day it will be depends on both the sun and the moon.

The earth spins on its axis, and as it spins it travels around the sun, a journey that takes a year. Twice each year, in spring and in autumn, the sun is directly over the imaginary line running around the widest part of the earth—the equator. At both these times, day and night are equal in length and we have an *equinox*. The spring equinox occurs around March 20, and the fall equinox around September 23.

6

Easter is always the first Sunday that follows the full moon on or after the spring equinox. The earliest date for Easter is March 22 and the latest April 25.

Forty days before Easter, not counting Sundays, there begins a religious season called *Lent,* which means lengthening days. On the first day of this season, Ash Wednesday, Catholic people have a cross marked on their forehead with ashes. It is a sign of their sorrow over their sins. In the Dark Ages only important people who had done something scandalous received ashes. These "public sinners" wore sackcloth and hair shirts, and went barefoot during Lent.

Lent recalls the forty days Jesus spent in the desert, fasting and becoming strong as he thought deeply about his work in the world. Serious Christians today look for ways during this time to become better and stronger, to make a fresh start. As a token, many give up certain pleasures or try to break bad habits during Lent.

The last week of Lent is called *Holy Week. Palm Sunday* is the first day. In many Christian churches everyone goes home with a frond of palm. This symbolizes the palms spread before Jesus as he rode into the city of Jerusalem just before his death. He had come there with his twelve disciples for the Passover, the Hebrew festival of freedom. Each year, at the first full moon of spring, the Hebrews, or Jews, celebrated the freeing of their ancestors from slavery in Egypt.

The Book of Exodus in the Bible tells the story. The evening before the Hebrews' flight from Egypt, the angel of God passed through the land. In every Egyptian home the angel destroyed the firstborn, but *passed over* the homes of the Hebrews.

From the old Hebrew word for Passover, *Pesach*, came the name for Easter in many languages, though not in English or German. In Spanish it is *Pascua*. The French word for Easter is *Pâques*, the Greek *Pascha*, and the Norwegian *Paaske*.

The fifth day of Holy Week is *Holy Thursday, Green Thursday, Maundy Thursday, Pure* or *Clean Thursday*. It honors the Lord's Supper, or Holy Communion, begun by a commandment of Jesus to his disciples the evening before he died. *Maundy* is from a Latin word meaning commandment. *Pure* and *Clean* come from a time when people could not wash or shave as often as now. On *Clean Thursday* they bathed and cleaned their whole bodies in preparation for Easter.

9

Good Friday is a day of mourning for Jesus' death.

Easter Eve, or *Holy Saturday,* is the last day before Easter. At some time during the day or evening, mourning for Jesus ends. Joyful celebrations begin at noontime or even before in countries like Spain or Mexico. Whistles blow, horns toot, and firecrackers explode. There may even be the booming of guns or a cannon.

Easter Sunrise

Long before there was a Christian religion or an Easter festival, man greeted spring with joyful celebrations. Winter was frightening. Each day the sun gave less warmth, less light, and stayed in the sky a shorter time. What if it slipped down behind a mountain or into the sea and never rose again?

But spring always returned. The sun grew brighter and each day was a little longer. Once again there would be fruits and flowers. Man and animals would thrive. Life would go on.

In their joy, people held spring festivals for the gods. Gathering around blazing bonfires, they chanted, danced, leapt through the flames, and made sacrifices. Sometimes there were cruel burnings as they celebrated the triumph of spring over winter, of life over death.

11

With bow and arrow and a few other simple tools, such early people lived by hunting and fishing. Roaming the forests and waterways, mountains and plains, they lived only from meal to meal.

Later, man learned to tame work animals and to grow crops. Now he could sow and reap, storing some of the food away.

Highest among the gods of these first farmers was the sun god who sent shining rays over the fields of grain. Sun worship reigned supreme.

Used to a sun god, many early Christians thought of Jesus as they had of the sun. Each evening the sun died and then rose to life again at dawn, they believed, just as Jesus was said to have died and risen. Thus sunrise became a symbol of the resurrection.

"The sun dances for joy at dawn on Easter, and a person seeing it will have good luck all year." There are still people in Europe who believe in this old saying. To anyone gazing straight at the sun, hoping with all his might, it really does seem to dance. No wonder that the belief was such a favorite for many years.

People often traveled long distances and waited, shivering in darkness and cold in order to be in a good spot to watch the Easter sunrise. Busy housewives, who could not leave their cottages, would try to catch the dancing rays of the Easter sun in a mirror or pan of water on the windowsill.

Today, every Easter, thousands of people all over our country and all over Europe still gather to watch the sunrise. In beautiful spots in towns or cities, in the mountains, or beside lakes, streams, and oceans, they attend special services.

The Easter sun in the United States comes first to Cadillac Mountain in Maine. From its summit, people see the sun rise out of the cold blue waters of the North Atlantic.

Then the sun moves westward to hundreds of other places where people are waiting —to the Garden of the Gods in the mountains of Colorado, to the Grand Canyon in Arizona, to the huge bowl-shaped crater of a dead volcano in the state of Hawaii.

Besides being a religious ceremony, watching the Easter sunrise has always been a way of expressing hope for a better life.

Even the name Easter has something to do with the sun. Some say it came down to us from the Norsemen's words *Eostur, Eastar, Ostara,* and *Ostar,* which meant season of the growing sun and season of new birth.

An old English history book by the scholar Bede tells of a goddess of dawn and springtime called *Eostre* who was worshiped by the Anglo-Saxon people of Europe before Christian times. Our word Easter may have come from her name; no one is really sure. We do know, though, that it refers to the East and the rising sun.

Easter Fire

The new Christian Church frowned on the gods of the pagans, as non-Christians were called. Spring fire rites to honor the sun god were forbidden until the year 752 A.D. By that time the pagan fires had changed into Easter fires. This is how it happened:

When Saint Patrick was a boy somewhere in what is now England or Scotland, he was captured by pirates from Ireland and taken there. For six years he tended sheep; then he escaped to France and became a monk. In 432 A.D. a vision led him back to Ireland to bring the Christian religion to the people.

Like other pagans, the Irish held spring fire rites, and did not want to give them up. So, in place of the old pagan custom, Patrick offered them a new Christian fire rite. On Easter Eve he gathered them together for huge bonfires outside the churches.

15

The custom of starting and blessing a new fire each year spread through Europe, and in time all Christian churches made it a part of the Easter service. Along with it there developed another custom. People would light a stick in the flames and take some of the precious Easter fire home with them.

As the years passed, they began preparing their homes for the new Easter fire in special ways. No fire or light burned in a house on Easter Saturday. All candlesticks, lamps, and stoves had to be clean and ready for the sacred fire.

During Easter week a boy in the family would place a log with others lying in a huge pile beside the church. Then, on Easter Eve the priest struck fire from flint, set the logs ablaze, and blessed the flames. Each boy found his own log and pulled it out by a wire he had left fastened to the end. Swinging it around in the air, he ran home.

With the burning log, his family would light all the lamps and candles and touch off the kindling in the fireplace or stove. The moment the kindling began to burn, they would snatch it from the fire, cool it, and put it away. Only when thunder and lightning threatened the house would the Easter kindling be burned again, as a magical charm.

In many European villages people still carry home sticks lighted at the new Easter fire. In others the Easter flames are often taken home in lanterns.

On Easter Eve, in parts of Germany, young people dance around blazing bonfires. They shout, sing Easter songs, leap over the flames, and sometimes set large straw wheels on fire and roll them down over the hillsides. The flaming wheel is a symbol of the sun, and the custom goes back to a time when most of mankind made a god of the sun.

Easter fires, like the sun from which they come, mean that life and light triumph over death and darkness.

Easter Candlelight

A lighted candle at Easter means the same thing as Easter sunrise or Easter fire: After darkness comes light, and after death, new life.

If you happened to be born into a Christian family in the United States, Easter morning might find you in a church where one tall white Paschal candle glows in the dimness. In many churches the candle is lighted on Easter Eve at a ceremony called "striking the new fire." The candle takes the place of the Easter fire of earlier times.

If your family belonged to a Greek Orthodox church, you would probably stay up all night on Easter Eve. At the stroke of midnight, with everybody else in your church, you would file out of a side door, with a lighted candle in

18

your hand. Back at the front door, one person would knock and ask, "Is Jesus in there?" From inside would come the answer, "No, he is not here. He has risen!" Then the door would open and everyone would troop back into the lighted church.

Candle ceremonies and processions have lighted Easter celebrations through the ages. In the early centuries of the Christian religion, people preparing to become members gathered in the church the afternoon before Easter. Each one in turn stood, pointed toward the sunset in the West, and promised to have nothing more to do with Satan, the prince of darkness. Then he pointed to the East, where the sun rises, and promised to follow Jesus, "the eternal light."

That night when the first star appeared, joyful singing and shouting began. Throughout a town or city, thousands of lamps and candles blazed forth. It seemed as bright as daytime. People looked forward eagerly to the glorious "night of light," and even the smallest children were allowed to stay up.

The Easter candlelight procession in Popayán, Colombia, once saved this tiny South American town from attack, so an old story goes. A fierce enemy tribe, coming down from the hills that night, saw an enormous fiery serpent winding toward them. The warriors halted. The townspeople, with their lighted candles, moved closer. In terror, the enemy fled.

Easter
Fireworks

If you lived in Florence, Italy, or visited there on Easter Saturday, you could join a crowd around an oxcart loaded with fireworks, standing ready beside a church. Suddenly a firecracker in the shape of a dove would fly out of the church window above, and run down over a wire to the oxcart. The fireworks would explode and the dove race back up the wire, into the church. If the bird reached the altar before exploding, there would be shouts of joy, and everybody present would expect good luck in the coming year.

In Taxco, Mexico, there is a reed structure one hundred feet high built especially to hold the Easter fireworks. Everybody gathers to watch. One firework sets off another, and as they explode in turn with beautiful colors, they form the shapes of crosses, animals, flowers, and birds.

In Italy, Spain, Portugal, throughout Latin America, and wherever there are Easter fireworks and firecrackers, their meaning is usually the same. The explosions of light and cheerful noise all express joy and are one more way of saying: Out of darkness comes light, and with it, new hope, and new life.

In Sweden, Easter firecrackers have a further meaning. Swedish children draw pictures of witches and write Easter greetings on them. Then, dressed up like witches themselves, they put their "Easter letters" in the mailboxes of their friends, and set off firecrackers in the street. The witches stand for evil spirits; the noisy firecrackers are meant to frighten them away.

Easter Eggs

Early man stared in wonder at an egg.

It looked like a stone. Then—crack! Out of the dead thing poked a tiny beak, a head, and the soft warm body of a living bird. It seemed a miracle—the miracle of new life.

This is the meaning of an Easter egg. It goes back far beyond any one religion and belongs to all mankind.

The ancient Egyptians, Persians, Phoenicians, and Hindus believed the world itself began with an enormous egg. In one Hindu myth the World Egg broke in two. Half turned to gold, becoming the sky, and half to silver, forming the earth. Mountains, rivers, and ocean, cloud and mists, came from layers just under the shell. And the being hatched from the giant egg became the sun.

An old story from Finland describes the creation of the world like this: Ukko, the highest god, sent the teal, a water bird, to nest on the knee of the great Water-Mother. From the broken eggs of the teal, earth and the heavens formed.

People of the Samoan Islands believed their great god Tangaloa-Langi hatched out of an egg himself. The broken bits of shell scattered and became their islands in the Pacific Ocean.

The ancient Persians, Greeks, and Chinese gave one another gifts of eggs during joyous spring festivals in celebration of the new life all around them. And today, when a new baby is born to Chinese parents, they share their happiness by sending a red egg to each relative and friend. The egg comes to a person's home like an announcement card.

The eggs of serpents were sacred to the ancient Druids, who lived in the forests and caves of England and France before Christian times. The Druids were sorcerers, priests, prophets, judges, and healers. They worshiped nature gods, practiced magic, and held secret ceremonies in sacred groves. In one of these

24

ceremonies, the Druids circled around a pile of serpent eggs. The eggs stood for life, while the circle meant that life is eternal—an endless chain.

No one is sure whether the idea of Easter eggs grew out of the World Egg of the ancient Egyptians, Persians, and peoples to the East, or how the idea may have traveled to the Western world. In earlier times not everything was written down, so many puzzles and mysteries remain.

The first book to mention Easter eggs by name was written five hundred years ago. Yet, a North African tribe that had become Christian long before that had a custom of coloring eggs at Easter. Clues like this make us think that Easter eggs began a very long time ago.

During the Middle Ages winters in northern Europe were very hard. Little food was left by spring. During Lent, besides giving up meat, people had to do without eggs. It was a religious custom and also a way of stretching meager food supplies a little further.

By Easter a fresh hen, duck, or goose egg was a precious thing indeed. Kings and nobles usually gave one to each of their castle servants as an Easter gift. Boys and girls who were lucky enough received a fresh egg for Easter, too. Hungry children would roam around at the Easter season, begging for them. Today children in some of the towns and villages in Europe still pass from house to house, asking for Easter eggs, just as American children pay trick-or-treat visits at Halloween.

English children call it Pace-egging. They recite special songs and verses such as this:

Please, Mrs. Whiteleg,
Please to give us an Easter egg,
If you won't give us an Easter egg,
Your hens will all lay addled eggs
And your cocks all lay stones.

Children of France repeat this little rhyme:

> I've a little cock in my basket
> It'll sing for you if you ask it
> With eggs red and white. Alleluia!

Dutch children in country places make wreaths of green with pastry chickens or stars tied to them. They carry their wreaths from house to house on Palm Sunday, begging for eggs and singing an old ditty that goes like this:

> Palm, Palm, Easter
> Hei Koeri.
> Soon it will be Easter,
> Then we will have an egg.
> One egg—two eggs,
> The third one is the Easter egg.

Baskets of eggs blessed at church on Easter Saturday became the special breakfast for Easter Sunday in Russia, the Ukraine, Poland, and the part of Europe that became Czechoslovakia. The custom grew up through the years and is still popular in many places today.

People everywhere came to believe in the magical powers of Easter eggs. "Painted eggs buried in the ground around Easter make grapevines grow well." This was a belief in countries like Yugoslavia, Bulgaria, and Greece. Something in the eggshells may have actually helped the growth of the vines by enriching the earth, but the people thought it happened because they were Easter eggs.

"The yolk of an egg laid on Good Friday and kept a hundred years will turn into a diamond." Among British people, this belief disappeared only a century ago.

Decorating eggs for Easter became an art, especially in eastern Europe. Often the eggs were dipped in red dye, but in Hungary there were more white ones with patterns of red flowers. Yugoslav people have usually marked their eggs with X V, standing for "Christ is risen."

Country people made their own Easter egg dyes. For the color yellow they boiled onion skins or hickory bark. For a light red they used madder root, while walnut shells or coffee gave them shades of brown. Sometimes they printed a lovely pattern on the shell of an egg by wrapping leaves and ferns around it before it was boiled.

Women and girls of Poland and the south of Russia always began working weeks ahead on eggs covered all over with designs. There would be lines that crisscrossed, tiny checkerboards, patterns of dots, and plant and animal shapes. No two eggs were alike but the same symbols appeared again and again. A sun was for good luck, a hen or rooster to make wishes come true, a deer for good health, and flowers for love and beauty.

The eggs were blessed at church and given to relatives and special friends to keep as souvenirs. Anyone with Russian or Polish friends may be lucky enough to see some of these beautiful Easter eggs. To many Russians and Poles leaving the old country, they were treasures too beautiful to leave behind.

The people we call the Pennsylvania Dutch brought with them from Germany the art of scratching designs on colored eggs. Their eggs are bright with tiny tulips, leaves, hearts, butterflies, and even elephants.

Wherever Easter is celebrated, there are egg games and egg contests. Players may roll hard-cooked eggs down a slope, each trying to have his own reach the bottom unbroken. Sometimes eggs are tossed into the air to see whose goes highest. Other egg games are like games of marbles. One player may aim his own egg at another as it lies on the ground, hoping to crack it. Or players may take turns rolling their eggs toward a hole in the ground, each trying to be the first there.

On the White House lawn in Washington, D. C., every year children roll eggs down over the grassy slopes in an Easter contest. A band plays, there are prizes, and the President of the United States is there.

Though the egg itself has a deeper meaning, the games are played mostly for fun. They express the joy of Easter. Once the games were more solemn. Several centuries ago, the bishop of Chester Cathedral in England took part in

30

an egg game. At certain times during the long Easter services there would be a recess while he and the choir singers played toss and catch with hard-boiled eggs. The eggs stood for the miracle of life just as they always have.

Chickens

King Akhnaton of ancient Egypt wrote a hymn to the sun. In it he said:

When the chicken chirps from
    within the shell
You give him breath that he may live
You bring his body to readiness
So that he may break from the egg.
And when he is hatched he runs on
    his two feet
Announcing his creation.

A newborn chicken meant the same thing to the Egyptians who worshiped the sun as it does in Easter celebrations today.

The chicken is a symbol of new life, like the egg, which is a chicken-to-be.

The Easter Rabbit

Children in Fredericksburg, Texas, have an Easter rabbit that is different from anyone else's. One Easter Eve in the nineteenth century when this town was first settled by German people, a family of children saw Indian campfires flaming on the hillsides all around. Their mother told them not to be afraid. It was just the Easter rabbit heating kettles of flower dye to color eggs. During the night, he would leave the eggs at the house for the children.

Every Easter Eve since, "rabbit fires" on the hilltops around Fredericksburg have lighted the whole town. And on Easter morning the children wake up to find colored eggs in nests made of bluebonnets and other Texas flowers.

Almost anywhere that Easter is celebrated there is an Easter bunny, though not always the same kind. Among the children in Panama, it is a painted rabbit called the *conejo* that brings the eggs.

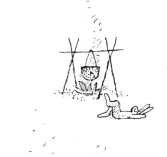

In countries where people speak German —Germany itself, Belgium, and Switzerland —children wait for *Oster Haas,* the Easter hare. The hare is larger and quicker than a rabbit, with longer legs and ears, and it does not dig a burrow in the ground like our cottontail.

The children often make pretty nests of leaves, moss, or grasses for the Easter hare, and sometimes special little gardens. Country children of Yugoslavia put their nests in the stable, while in England they hide them in the garden or around the house.

Many Indian tribes in Central American countries like Guatemala believe in the Christian religion now, but they have woven into Easter celebrations bits of the ancient springtime festivals of their ancestors. They build Easter arches covered with flowers, fruits, vegetables, and stuffed small animals of the fields and forests—squirrels, raccoons, and rabbits.

Everyone knows what large families rabbits have, and how fast the little bunnies grow up and have babies of their own, until there

are more and more and more. And most people believe that the hare or rabbit of Easter is a symbol of new life, as it probably was in religions far older than Christianity.

The Easter Lamb

The little lambs on Easter cards, toy lambs, and lambs made of candy or pastry go back far beyond Easter to the first Passover of the Jewish people.

It was at the time their ancestors were slaves in Egypt. Before the angel of God took the firstborn in all Egyptian homes, the Hebrew leader Moses ordered a sacrifice. Every Hebrew family was to sprinkle the blood of a young lamb over its doorframe. The lamb had to be roasted and eaten, together with bread baked without yeast, and bitter herbs. If this was done, Moses said, the angel would pass over their homes, and bring them no harm.

Hebrew people who joined the Christian

religion in its early years brought with them the traditions of their ancient Passover festival. One of these was the sacrifice of a lamb. Gradually, as some of the older ways blended with the Christian customs, the lamb took on a different meaning. In the Hebrew religion the lamb's life was a sacrifice to God. To the Christians the life of Jesus was the sacrifice. The lamb became an Easter lamb, a symbol of Jesus.

Poems, stories, and hymns often call Jesus The Lamb of God. But sometimes he is The Good Shepherd with mankind as his flock. Many pictures show Jesus with a shepherd's staff, carrying a little lamb.

Besides its religious meaning, the Easter lamb has others given to it by shepherds and farmers in earlier days. They believed it was good luck to meet a lamb, particularly during the Easter season. If you looked from your window on Easter Sunday and saw a lamb, you could expect even better luck, especially if its nose happened to be pointing toward your house. The reason given was that the devil could take any form but that of a dove or a lamb.

36

For many centuries, all Christians who could obtain it ate roast lamb for their Easter dinner. In Italy and countries to the East, lamb is still the favorite meat for this holiday. In other parts of Europe a mound of butter in the shape of a lamb sometimes appears on the dinner table. Often the centerpiece is a sugar or pastry lamb, surrounded with green leaves.

An Easter Animal Parade

All Herds and Flocks
Rejoice, all Beasts of thickets and of rocks.
—*Christina G. Rossetti*

Baby chicks, bunnies, and lambs are Easter animals we know well. Other creatures that have come and gone through centuries of celebrations would make a long Easter parade. In the front ranks would march a lion, a butterfly, and a whale.

37

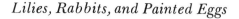

At one time, people thought that a lion cub was born dead. Three days later the father lion breathed life into the baby lion, they believed.

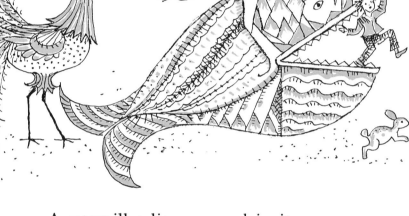

A caterpillar lies wrapped in its cocoon like a dead object. Then, as if by magic, a beautiful butterfly flutters forth.

Jonah, in the Bible story, spent three days and nights in the belly of a whale, then came out, alive!

To the early Christians these creatures were like their Jesus, who died and rose again to life.

In earlier times two beautiful birds were also Easter symbols—a real bird, the peacock, and a bird of myth and legend, the phoenix.

38

The peacock, with its beautiful fan of green and blue feathers, becomes a new bird each spring. Shedding its old feathers, it parades majestically in brilliant new ones.

The phoenix, a fabulous bird like an eagle, but with feathers of red and gold, may never have existed at all. In stories and legends the phoenix was said to live for five hundred years. Then, fanning its golden wings, it would set its nest afire and die. From the ashes would rise a new phoenix. In ancient Egypt the phoenix was a symbol of the sun, which seemed to die each night and come to life again at dawn.

To early Christians, both the peacock and the phoenix were symbols of new life arising from old—the resurrection.

39

Hot Cross Buns

Every year when Lent begins, the delicious spicy bun with raisins inside and a shiny brown top decorated with a cross of white icing appears again. The story of hot cross buns goes so far back that no one is sure where it begins.

One belief goes like this: Every year the ancient Anglo-Saxons baked small wheat cakes in honor of their goddess of springtime, Eostre. Even after they became Christians, they continued this old custom. The church looked for a way to make them give up the pagan goddess. It decreed that, in place of the cakes honoring Eostre, there would be others sacred to the Christian festival held at the same time of year.

If this was the beginning of hot cross buns, they are really far older than Christianity itself. As for the cross on top, this was a pagan symbol long before the birth of Jesus Christ. The same mark appeared on cakes sacred to Diana, the Roman goddess of the moon and of hunting.

40

A monk in England baked hot cross buns and gave them to the poor at the Easter season six hundred years ago, according to one old account. The monk may have been baking the first hot cross buns or he may have been carrying on a custom that had started earlier. We cannot be sure.

No matter how it started, baking and eating hot cross buns as Easter drew near was a custom that everyone enjoyed. In England housewives rose before daylight on Good Friday to bake the buns for their families. Bakers stayed at their ovens all night. Street vendors with trays shouted:

Hot cross-buns, hot cross-buns,
One a penny, two a penny, hot
                        cross-buns;
Smoking hot, piping hot,
Just come out of the baker's shop;
One a penny poke, two a penny tongs,
Three a penny fire-shovel, hot cross-buns!

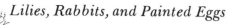

All sorts of ideas grew up about the magic powers of hot cross buns. If you ate them on Good Friday, people said, your home would be safe from fire all year. Some of the buns they put back into the oven to harden and keep. They would grate the hardened buns to take as medicine, use them as charms against lightning, and hang them from the ceiling to bring good luck to the house. Farmers believed a dried hot cross bun would keep rats out of their cornfields. Sailors took them to sea to keep the ship from being wrecked.

Other special breads and cakes are symbols of Easter in various countries. People in Czechoslovakia eat Easter *babovka,* a delicious coffee bread. Polish people have *baba,* a cake-like bread in the shape of an old peasant woman's full skirts. The Greeks and Portuguese eat a round flat loaf marked with a cross and decorated with Easter eggs. Christians in Syria and Jordan have special honey pastries for the holiday. Italians bake a pizza made with eggs especially for Easter—not the pizza of the United States, with tomato and cheese on top, but a bread.

If you stare at a pretzel and use plenty of

imagination, you may be able to see the shape of a person with his arms folded, praying. This is what the first pretzels were meant to be. Monks at the Vatican in Rome made them to give to the poor in the fifth century after Christ. For a long time afterward, pretzels were a symbol of Lent just as hot cross buns are today. In Austria, they were hung on palm branches on Palm Sunday.

Easter Colors

The colors most often used in Easter decorations—white, yellow or gold, and delicate shades of green and purple—are the colors of springtime, too. They are the colors of new leaves and grass, spring flowers, flowering shrubs and trees.

White stands for light, purity, and joy.

We see it in Easter candles, in the fragrant Easter lily, and combined with the pastel colors of Easter.

Yellow stands for sunlight and radiance, and is also the color for April, the month in which Easter most often comes.

For several hundred years after Jesus Christ, sun worship and the worship of the Christian god went on side by side. So the early Christians saw their new god in the same way they had seen the sun—as a glorious light shining over the world.

Radiance was a symbol of earthly kings as well as of the divine or heavenly one. Light

44

seemed to shine on the royal person and to radiate from his golden crown. And Jesus is often called prince.

These are some of the reasons that artists of all ages have shown Jesus with a halo of light around his head.

Purple is a royal color, too. And in the language of religious symbols it stands for mourning. Purple draperies cover the statues and pictures in some of the Christian churches during Lent to show sorrow over Jesus' death. In Catholic churches purple decorates the altar during solemn Holy Week services.

The purple dye of the ancient world came from a certain shellfish in the Mediterranean Sea. Since each fish gave but a speck, it was a dye only the wealthiest could afford. No wonder that purple garments and the color itself became the mark of kings and emperors.

Green stands for nature and for hope of eternal life.

When green colored the bare tree branches and spread over the fields in spring, early pagan peoples took hope. A new year was beginning for all living and growing things.

45

In some countries the Thursday before Easter is called Green Thursday. Priests of the Middle Ages wore green robes on this day. Wrongdoers who were being pardoned at this time also wore green or carried sprigs of green plants.

At home people had their own customs for the day. They ate green foods—herb soup, spinach, served with eggs, and green salads. Not to do so was bad luck, they came to believe. Among German people an old saying warns that a person who refuses to eat the green salad may turn into a donkey. And while no one today believes such a thing, the custom of green foods for Green Thursday still goes on in a large part of Europe.

Easter Bells

Sometimes on Easter Saturday but by Sunday morning at the latest, bells ring forth in church steeples. Fasting and mourning are over. It is time for the joyful part of the festival.

Bells have called people to church and have sounded the hours for centuries. And through the years peasants came to believe that the bells, like the noise of a gun or cannon, frightened evil spirits away.

In countries like France and Italy the bells are silent from Holy Thursday until Easter Sunday. In Germany and central Europe even the bells on farm buildings are still, though there they begin to ring again on Holy Saturday.

With the bells silent, the farm people of the Middle Ages felt uneasy. So, to comfort themselves and their children, they would say, "The bells have flown to Rome, but they'll come back for Easter."

47

To this day small children of Germany and central Europe are told that the church bells have gone to Rome to visit the Pope or one of the holy tombs. Small French children believe the bells fly to Rome and find Easter eggs for those who have behaved well through the year.

In towns and villages where the bells start ringing on Holy Saturday, people at home listen for them. At the sudden pealing, they hug and kiss and wish one another a happy Easter.

In the Greek Orthodox Church the bells start pealing at the moment in the midnight service when the church door opens to the procession of people with lighted candles.

Slavic countries like Poland, Russia, and the Ukraine had a custom which lingers on in many places. There, the bells ring from morning till night, with short pauses in between, to remind everyone that Easter is the greatest church festival.

48

People in Austria and Germany like their old custom of striking the hours with wooden clappers instead of bells. Every hour, from Holy Thursday evening on, boys pass through a town or village with their clappers, singing old Easter carols, a different stanza each time. One of the Easter songs begins like this:

We beg you, people, hear and hark!
It's nine o'clock, and fully dark.

Today, in our own country, cheerful Easter bells are often all that remains of the noisier, more lively celebrations of earlier times and other parts of the world.

49

Easter Flowers and Plants

A hard brown bulb with a papery shell is buried in earth. Soon a beautiful white Easter lily grows and blossoms.

Lilies and other flowers that grow from bulbs, such as tulips or daffodils, are symbols of the resurrection. The bulb stands for the tomb of Jesus, the blossom for his life after death.

The early spring narcissus of the Alps, with its white or yellow blossoms, has been an Easter flower for centuries. And long before Christian times the same flower was part of a Greek myth about springtime and the changing seasons.

The goddess Persephone of the myth was in a meadow picking flowers. Suddenly, dozens of narcissus burst into blossom from a plant at her feet. As she reached to pick them, the earth opened and Pluto, the god of the under-world, appeared in his black chariot. He took Persephone with him to his underground kingdom. There, she was forced to live ever afterward for six months of every year. While she was underground, her mother Demeter mourned for her and it was wintertime. When she returned to the world, spring returned with her.

The fragrant, waxy white flower we call the Easter lily is not a spring flower or an American flower at all. A lily growing on islands near Japan was taken to Bermuda and then traveled to the United States to become our most special Easter plant. Flower growers have learned how to make it bloom in time.

Christian people of Iraq, in the Middle East, make their homes beautiful for the holiday with wild tulips they call lilies of the field. People of England and Russia have always picked pussy willows for Easter. Mexican children and grownups gather armloads of bright tropical flowers and take them to church to be blessed.

No matter what the Easter flower or plant is, it stands for *all* flowers and *all* plants. Any of the green growing things of the earth stand for new life and new hope—the smallest dandelion blossom picked in a vacant lot or beside a road, or the tallest Easter lily from a greenhouse.

Before Christian times people believed trees and plants had a magical power which turned them green in springtime. The touch of a leafy branch at this season was supposed to bring good health and good luck. Gently switching another person with a green branch was a way of wishing him the same. Sometimes the branch was called "the rod of life." And a youth or maiden tapped with the rod was expected to become a strong and healthy grownup, blessed with children.

52

People joining the Christian religion when it was new brought along with them springtime ideas and customs like these. Because the church's Easter festival came in the spring, too, they began to think of them as Easter customs. In time it was forgotten that they had ever been anything else.

Switching still goes on in Europe, usually on the day after Easter. Where the pussy willow grows, men and boys tap the women and girls with a branch of it, sometimes decorated with flowers and ribbons. In Austria the country people call it the "stroke of health." In Poland and Czechoslovakia, it is the "willow switch."

Easter Water

Drenching another person with water on Easter Monday is one more custom that goes back to the days before Christianity. In those times people believed that water, like plants, had special powers. Year after year they watched, amazed, as solid ice on rivers and ponds turned back into water in the spring. Surely anything so magical as water could make them stronger and more powerful. Each spring, as soon as the ice melted, the people bathed in the icy water and sprinkled their farm animals with it.

Children loved games of splashing water on one another then just as they do today. But in those times grownups took part in them, too. They believed the splashing would bring them good luck and good health.

The church frowned on such pagan customs, but the old belief in the magic power of water in springtime was strong. To turn a pagan custom into a Christian one, priests began to bless all streams and ponds in a neighborhood at the Easter season. Before long people would wait for the blessing of the waters before taking their spring baths. And they began to save water dipped up on Easter for its special healing powers.

Among young girls the idea sprang up that the Easter water would make them beautiful. Girls who did not live near a brook or pond would steal outdoors early on Easter morning to wash their faces in dew.

"Drenching" or "dousing" still goes on in Europe today centuries after it first became an Easter custom. Boys enjoy dousing girls with buckets or bottles of water, teasing them and saying special rhymes. Children in costumes visit farms and recite ditties. At the end they splash a little water on the farmer's wife and receive a treat of eggs or sweets. In some of the cities of Europe the old custom has changed a little. People politely squirt a little perfume at one another and exchange wishes for good luck through the year.

The French people of Canada still wash with water from rivers or fountains that have been blessed on Easter. Some of them believe the water will heal them of sickness, and they keep bottles of it to use during the year.

In Germany and Austria a bride and groom often sprinkle each other with Easter water on their wedding day for health and good luck. And there are still farmers in Europe who sprinkle their animals with water drawn from springs and brooks during the Easter season.

Water is not an Easter symbol that we notice as we do the eggs and chickens, the bunnies and baskets, and flowers of Easter. But it is an important and ancient symbol of the holiday. In many churches babies are baptized with water during the Easter season.

Easter Clothes

Where winters are cold, everybody likes to shed heavy winter things for lighter, more cheerful spring clothes. But people who celebrate Easter often save their new shoes, suits, dresses, coats, and especially their new "Easter bonnets" for the holiday. In their new clothes, they go to church and stroll in parks or along sidewalks.

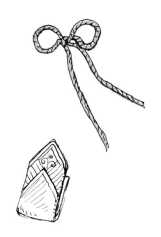

In cities like New York, the Easter Parade of people dressed up in spring finery has become an event to be watched. Among the throng are men in top hats and tail coats, and ladies in hats that are like huge baskets of flowers, fruits, or berries worn upside down. Onlookers watch for noted actors and actresses, men and women known for their great wealth, or famous in other ways. Newsmen take pictures for papers, magazines, and television.

It is sometimes said that people who parade on Easter to show off their new clothes have forgotten the meaning of the holiday. But the custom really began a very long time ago and has deep meaning.

In the first few centuries after Jesus, new members of the church were baptized in water the week before Easter. The fresh white robes they wore after their baptism gave us the name White Week, by which Holy Week is still known in some places.

More centuries passed. Christians grew in numbers, and Easter became a more and more important festival. By the Middle Ages a person was expected to dress in fresh clothing at Easter, whether he was newly baptized or not. Most people were poor and wore the same clothes all winter, one layer over another. Only the most fortunate had enough layers to keep them warm.

At the Easter season, usually on "Pure Thursday," people took off their winter clothes for the first time in many months, and bathed their bodies in the icy ponds and streams. Anyone lucky enough to have something new to wear put it on. The others dressed in their old clothes that had been freshly washed.

People wanted their houses to be ready for Easter, too. They cleaned the soot and ashes of winter out of the fireplaces that had kept the family warm. They swept the hearth for the holiday and laid fresh flowers and green rushes on the clean stones.

After the Easter church service people young and old, dressed in their fresh Easter clothes, went on a special walk together through the town, into the fields and woodlands. At certain spots they stopped to pray and sing Easter hymns. At the head of the procession there was usually someone carrying a lighted candle. Young farmers of Germany and Austria liked to deck out their horses in flowers, leaves, and ribbons and ride them in the Easter procession.

In time the Easter walks became less and less religious. But people kept on dressing up and taking walks as part of the celebration. In countries like Poland they call these Emmaus Walks, and there are Emmaus Groves where picnics are held on Easter Monday. The name comes from the Bible story of two friends of Jesus who met him on the road to Emmaus after he had risen to life again.

Through the years all sorts of beliefs about Easter clothes sprang up. Not to wear something new was "bad luck." Even the poorest man or boy would try to have at least a new shoestring. A girl too poor to have anything more would usually find a bit of new ribbon for her hair or her hat.

A young man who liked a girl might give her a new pair of gloves. If she wore them on Easter Sunday it meant that she liked him, too. Sometimes it meant that they were engaged to be married.

Sing, Creatures, sing,
Angels and Men and Birds and everything.
—*Christina G. Rossetti*

New clothes, a newborn chicken, a lily, an egg, an exploding firecracker—these and the many other symbols of Easter all really say the same thing, each in a little different way.

The sun sets and there is darkness, but at dawn there is new light, a fresh start.

Trees and plants die, but from their seeds new plants spring up. Man and other animals die, too, but leave others like themselves behind.

In winter the earth itself may seem to die, then come to life again in spring. In springtime all living things are just beginning or beginning again.

61

No matter what a person's religion, these are joyful thoughts, shared by people everywhere—people of today as well as those who lived long before there was a Christian religion at all. For Easter is a religious holiday and also much more. It is a festival of hope, of awakening life, and of man's joy in being alive.

Other Easter Books

FISHER, Aileen. Illustrated by Ati Forberg. *Easter*. New York: Thomas Y. Crowell Co., 1968. Includes the story of the first Easter as well as customs through history, and ways of celebrating Easter today. For younger children to read by themselves.

HARPER, Wilhelmina, compiler. *Easter Chimes: Stories for Easter and the Spring Season*. New York: E. P. Dutton Co., rev. ed., 1965. Stories, poems, and legends of Easter and springtime for children of all ages by such authors as Hans Christian Andersen, Padraic Colum, and Oscar Wilde, as well as Easter customs around the world. Suitable for schools, libraries, and homes.

HAZELTINE, Alice I., and Smith, Elva S., editors. *The Easter Book of Legends and Stories*. New York: Lothrop, Lee & Shepard Co., 1944. Seventy selections, including poems as well as stories and legends in a wide range.

HOLE, Christina. *Easter and Its Customs*. New York: Barrows, 1961. Easter customs through the centuries, including many interesting and little-known facts. For children of nine and up or for adults who read to children.

ICKIS, Marguerite. *The Book of Festival Holidays*. New York: Dodd Mead & Co., 1964. The Easter chapter includes an Easter song, ways of decorating eggs, Easter egg games, Easter favors made from eggshells, music and instructions for an Easter egg dance. For children of eight years and up or adults who work with them.

MILHOUS, Katherine. Story and pictures by the author. *The Egg Tree*. New York: Charles Scribner's Sons, 1950. The Caldecott Award winning story based on a Pennsylvania Dutch egg tree Easter custom.

SOCKMAN, Ralph W. *Easter Story for Children*. Nashville: Abingdon Press, 1966. The story of Jesus, from birth through the crucifixion and resurrection. For younger children.

YATES, Elizabeth. *Easter Story*. New York: E. P. Dutton Co., rev. ed., 1967. A story which weaves in many Easter customs and traditions. For children of ten years and up.

63

Index

COMMUNITY LIBRARY ASS'N
Ketchum, Idaho